WELCOME TO
PASSPORT TO READING
A beginning reader's ticket to a brand-new world!

Every book in this program is designed to build read-along and read-alone skills, level by level, through engaging and enriching stories. As the reader turns each page, he or she will become more confident with new vocabulary, sight words, and comprehension.

These PASSPORT TO READING levels will help you choose the perfect book for every reader.

READING TOGETHER
Read short words in simple sentence structures together to begin a reader's journey.

READING OUT LOUD
Encourage developing readers to sound out words in more complex stories with simple vocabulary.

READING INDEPENDENTLY
Newly independent readers gain confidence reading more complex sentences with higher word counts.

READY TO READ MORE
Readers prepare for chapter books with fewer illustrations and longer paragraphs.

This book features sight words from the educator-supported Dolch Sight Words List. This encourages the reader to recognize commonly used vocabulary words, increasing reading speed and fluency.

For more information, please visit passporttoreadingbooks.com.

Enjoy the journey!

Little, Brown and Company

Hachette Book Group
1290 Avenue of the Americas, New York, NY 10104
Visit us at lb-kids.com

Little, Brown and Company is a division of Hachette Book Group, Inc. The Little, Brown name and logo are trademarks of Hachette Book Group, Inc.

The publisher is not responsible for websites (or their content) that are not owned by the publisher.

First Edition: April 2016

Library of Congress Control Number: 2016932124

ISBN 978-0-316-27143-1

10 9 8 7 6 5 4 3 2

CW

Printed in the United States of America

Passport to Reading titles are leveled by independent reviewers applying the standards developed by Irene Fountas and Gay Su Pinnell in *Matching Books to Readers: Using Leveled Books in Guided Reading*, Heinemann, 1999.

CAPTAIN AMERICA

WE ARE THE AVENGERS

Adapted by A. Harrison Smith

Illustrated by Ron Lim, Andy Smith, and Andy Troy

Based on the screenplay by Christopher Markus
and Stephen McFeely

Produced by Kevin Feige

Directed by Anthony and Joe Russo

LITTLE, BROWN AND COMPANY
New York   Boston

Attention, Captain America fans!
Look for these words
when you read this book.
Can you spot them all?

shield

wings

mask

tube

The Avengers are Earth's Mightiest Heroes! They fight in many battles.

They work together as a team, and keep the world safe.

Steve Rogers is Captain America.

He is the leader of the Avengers.

His shield can stop almost anything.

Tony Stark is Iron Man.
His metal suit is very strong.
He can fly through the air.

Natasha Romanoff is the Black Widow.

She is a super-spy.

She can move fast and fight hard.

Steve, Tony, and Natasha go on many missions.
Now the Avengers have some new team members!

11

Scarlet Witch can float in the air. She can move things with her mind and has special powers.

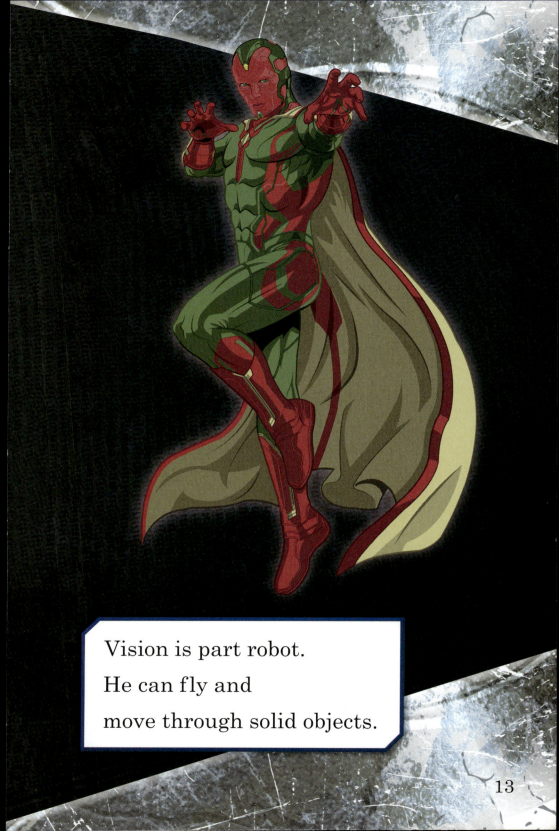

Vision is part robot.

He can fly and

move through solid objects.

War Machine has an iron suit.

He can fire missiles, just like Iron Man.

Falcon has metal wings.
He can swoop through the air
like a bird.

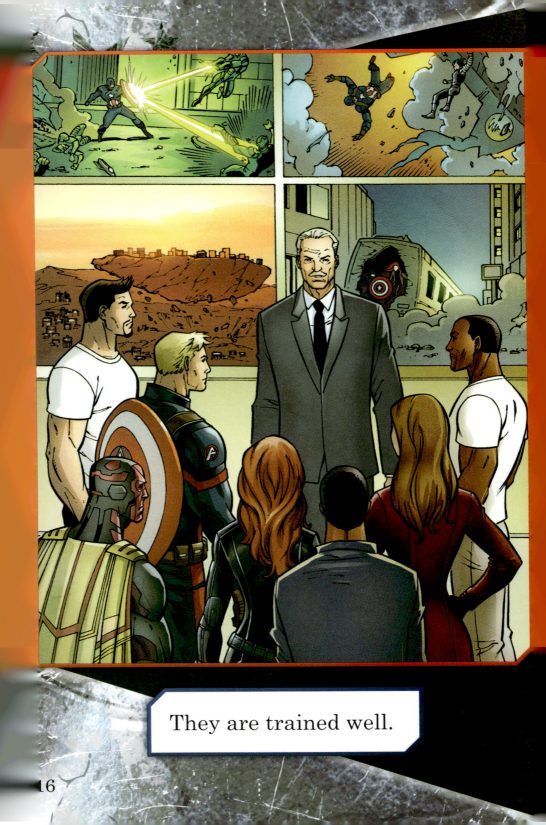

They are trained well.

Now the new team must save the day!

Crossbones was a S.H.I.E.L.D. agent. He worked with Steve.

Now he is very dangerous. He wears a skull mask and can punch hard!

Crossbones and his gang
try to steal a test tube.
It contains a virus that could hurt people.

Captain America, Black Widow,
Scarlet Witch, and Falcon
must stop them.
But there is an explosion.
BOOM!

Crossbones leaps down
and attacks, but he is no match for Cap!

His team helps, too.

Black Widow finds the test tube.

Falcon joins the fight from above.

SWOOSH!

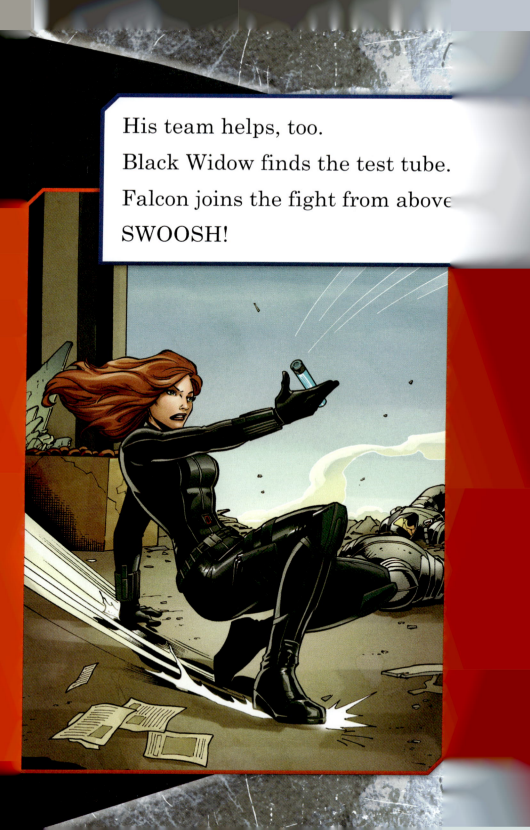

There are always new battles to fight when you are an Avenger!

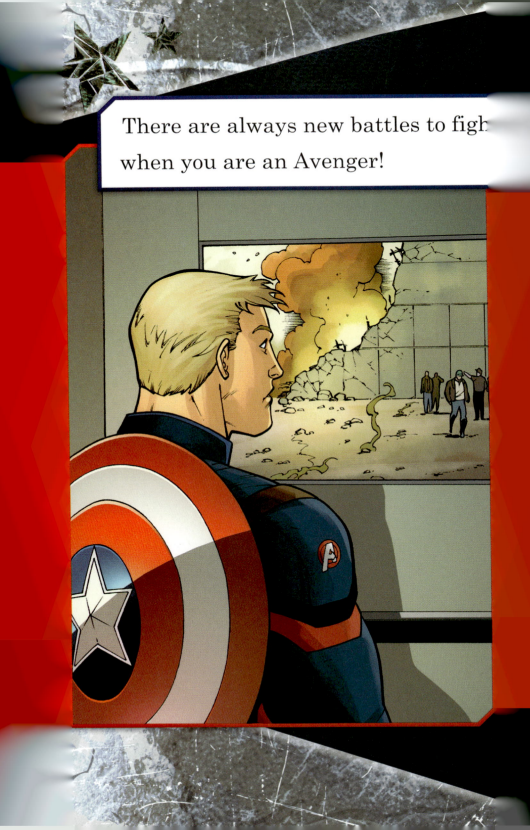

Bucky Barnes used to be Cap's friend.
Now he is the Winter Soldier.
He has a metal arm and is very strong!

Cap is looking for Bucky, but he is not the only one.

Black Panther is also on the hunt.
He wears body armor
and a mask that has catlike ears.

Black Panther attacks Bucky.
They fight hard!

Falcon and Cap jump in, but Black Panther is very strong. His claws scratch Cap's shield!

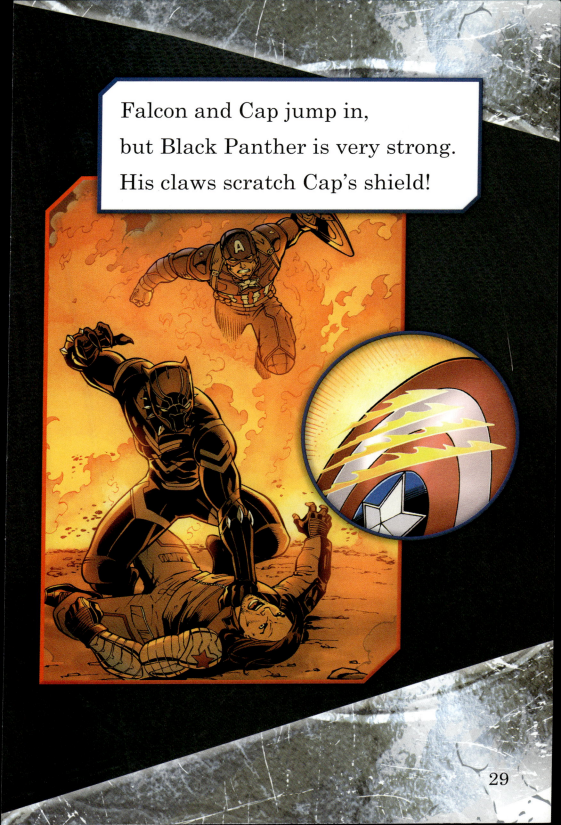

War Machine arrives just in time!
He fires missiles.

The fight ends, and Bucky is captured.